ARCHIE'S 7-DAY MILE

Steve Lovett

Wrate's Publishing

First published 2019 by Wrate's Publishing

ISBN 978-1-9996089-1-0

Copyright © Steve Lovett, 2019

Edited and typeset by Wrate's Editing Services
www.wrateseditingservices.co.uk

This book is a work of fiction.

Names, characters, places and incidents are either a product of the author's imagination or are used fictitiously. Any resemblance to actual people living or dead, events or locales is entirely coincidental.

A CIP catalogue record for this book is available from the British Library.

Printed and bound by CPI Group (UK) Ltd, Croydon, CRO 4YY

ARCHIE'S 7-DAY MILE

PROLOGUE

Many years ago, a colony of creatures travelled from a distant planet. Rocketing through the solar system, their engines whined and spluttered. With a flaming red tail the spaceship streaked through the Earth's atmosphere and into angry, dark clouds. Ravaged by thunder the ship floundered and hundreds of parachutes launched off the craft and into a cyclone.

Blown to every continent, the blue-green aliens, who were only the size of a bug and walked on two legs, began a new life in the wondrous realm of the insects. (The world of insects is similar to our own but their achievements go unnoticed.) Towns and villages spread across the globe, unseen by humans, as their natural camouflage concealed their buildings and triumphs from view.

CHAPTER 1

Archie skipped along the cobbled avenue towards the village noticeboard. He'd heard rumours of a new poster asking for competitors for a world record attempt. But it couldn't be true, could it?

He slowed and, weaving between dandelions poking through the cobbles, watched a wasp land in front of the noticeboard.

"Wow, it's true," he said, and read out loud from the illuminous yellow poster. "Contestants wanted for the first ever seven-day land mile attempt. First place, a world trip for two."

The wasp laughed and glanced at Archie. "You land stompers couldn't manage a whole mile in seven weeks, let alone seven days," he said, before launching himself into the air.

Archie tipped his head. "You could be right," he said, "but what an adventure it would be!"

Archie thought about the poster for the rest of the day. *Is it possible?* he wondered. *Could a mile on land be completed in only seven days?*

❦❦❦

That evening, as the full moon peaked high in the sky, Archie's family grew quiet in anticipation of the evening's story time. Slumped on the rose-petal sofa with Archie were his mother, father, his brother Rew and his sisters, Hester and Ula.

Archie's father commenced. "Many seasons ago, Great-Uncle Silas . . ." The story went on. You could have heard a butterfly flutter. From his position at the end of the sofa, Archie stared at the moss carpet and shuffled his hands and feet. He sighed. *Could I do a mile in just seven days?* he asked himself. *It would be such an adventure!* "Yes!" he shouted out loud. "Yes I can!"

"What do you mean, 'yes I can'?" asked his father.

Archie stood up and told his family about the poster.

"But you never finish anything you start," stated his father.

"You gave up on the one-metre race last year," said his brother Rew.

His sisters said nothing, but pointed at an unfinished jigsaw collecting dust on the table.

"Oh, Archie, they're right," said his mother, as she stood up. "You don't finish anything. What makes you think you could do a mile in seven days?"

"I can do it, I know I can. I'll train every day – it would be a world record and I could be an adventurer, just like Great-Uncle Silas."

Early the next morning, Archie crept down the stairs, jumping over the bottom step, which he knew always creaked. He tiptoed across the carpet and out of the door. Met by the cool, crisp morning air, he took a deep breath and ran out of the close towards the village.

This is easy, he thought. He passed the post office and started up the small hill by the school. Almost halfway up, he gasped; every new breath sounded like a faulty whistle. Overtaken by a really old cricket with two walking sticks, he put his hands to his knees and continued, eventually leaving the village behind.

After many hours, Archie winced and hobbled to a stop. He decided that at the very least he must have run 100-metres. He turned, gawped at the road sign and then scratched his head and said, "I don't believe it, all that effort for a 10-metre run!" He sighed and his tummy felt like it was sinking. There was nothing to do but limp back to the village.

Almost home, he heard the sound of familiar whispers. He looked up and saw his brother, sisters and a group of friends sitting on top of a straw fence.

"Given up already?" asked Tombo, one of his friends.

"You won't even make it to the stadium," joked another mate, William.

"You're a world record holder already," his sister Hester shouted, "for not finishing anything!"

"Archie, the dreamer," ranted Rew.

"I'm not going to cry," whispered Archie to himself. Taking a big breath, he put his hands over his ears, looked forward, opened his eyes as wide as possible, and headed home.

That evening, Archie clambered the twisted willow ladder of his bunk and, sinking into the soft grass mattress, looked through the moonlit window above. Forcing out a yawn, he gazed at the star-filled sky and started counting . . . one, two, three . . . but it was no good, time felt frozen. The village clock chimed midnight and, wriggling around the bed, Archie sighed, clenched his fists and said out loud, "I'll show them. I'm no dreamer, I can do it. I'm sure I can, can't I?"

CHAPTER 2

After weeks of training, the time came for Archie to set off for the City and the famous Green Leaf Stadium. Leaving Rew asleep in the bottom bunk, he stepped onto the landing and stopped at the door of his sisters' bedroom. Both of them were asleep, so Archie continued down the landing before hesitantly turning back as a single tear fell from his face.

"B . . . b . . . bye," he said.

He looked through heavy eyes to see his mother and father waiting at the bottom of the stairs.

"There's my boy," said his mum. "Oh, my beautiful son, you will be careful." She wrapped her arms around Archie and squeezed him tight.

"Of course I will, Mother."

Archie's father handed him a bright green rucksack made from a pea pod. "Now, don't look inside it until you're in the stadium."

Archie said goodbye and made his way towards the gate. He turned to give one final wave and heard his father shout. "Prove us all wrong. Make your own adventure, Archie, and give us a new story to tell."

"I . . . I will, Father, bye-bye."

Archie slouched on a stone. He'd been walking for days now and the vine laces in his tatty leaf-shoes had frayed from where they had dragged on the ground. Clasping the laces, he felt the ground tremble and heard a buzz.

Vroom!

Leaving the swarm, a wasp dived towards Archie, landed on a bright dandelion and turned around. "I can't believe it's you. You're that land stomper from Blossomville."

Archie's antenna turned crimson. Biting his lip, he lifted his head and said, "Be careful, you almost hit me."

"You're not seriously going to do the race, are you? Those little feet of yours will barely make it to the City. No, what you need for distance is wings."

Archie watched the wasp fly away and over an enormous wooden fence. Maybe he was right. He looked at his feet, sighed and remembered all the other taunts. His head drooped and his arms hung by his side. "No," he said out loud, "I can't give up. I won't be known as Archie the quitter."

❧ ❧ ❧

The moon peeped out from behind a cloud, as Archie navigated the narrow path up Rockery Pass. The summit felt like metres away and every corner was met by another steep incline.

"I'm never going to make it to the top," Archie said out loud.

Trudging forward, the summit came into view with an unfamiliar glow against the backdrop of the dark sky. Archie shuffled forward then gasped. Hundreds of city lights glittered like stars on the horizon.

The next morning, he rolled from under a faded tulip petal, yawned and rubbed from his eyelids a wet, sticky collection of dust and mud. Still a day's hike away from the City, he flung the pea-pod rucksack over his shoulder and made his way towards the lush green valley below.

After a day on his feet, Archie finally reached the City. "Wow!" he muttered, as he strolled through the arch of the clock tower. He'd never seen such an assortment of shops, cafés and bars, which lined the bustling plaza. Taking a breath, he stepped back and watched a group of flying fleas perform acrobatics. Each time they propelled upwards, they were briefly bathed in an orange glow from the dimming evening sun.

Archie saw a flash and turned towards it. An enormous mushroom had been lit up by hundreds of glittering bulbs that hung from under its curved top. Dazzled, he rubbed his eyes then watched fifty more mushrooms light up in sequence, snaking either side of Green Leaf Way.

Leaving the plaza, Archie joined the crowd heading up to the stadium. Close to the top, he leaned against the leathery stem of a mushroom and took in the vista over the City.

Then he heard, "On three . . . one, two, three."

Archie looked over his shoulder to see several aphids in white coats pushing a snail up the hill.

Archie continued, before turning to look at the snail, "At least he won't be in the race, will he?" he said out loud.

Strolling over the crest of the hill, Green Leaf Stadium came into view. The exquisitely designed oak walls, made from a converted tree stump, rose majestically towards the sky. Archie gazed up at the massive stadium, cupped both of his hands, closed his eyes and said quietly to himself, "Yes, I've made it this far."

CHAPTER 3

Sitting alone in a dimly lit waiting room, Archie's tummy felt tight. Every second felt like a minute and each minute an hour. *Have I been forgotten?* he wondered. Fidgeting, he heard the increasing sound of voices and the clattering of thousands of feet.

"It can't be long now," he said to himself. Every few seconds he looked to the door, hoping the handle would drop. Tingling all over, he launched himself off the bench. Landing, he did the splits and tore his leaf-shoes completely in two.

"Oh, no!" he cried.

He shook his head. What was he going to do now?

Gradually getting to his feet, he hopped to the bench. "It's going to be a long walk home," he said out loud. "At least they can't say I didn't make it to the stadium."

Holding his breath, he scrunched up his eyes, as tears burst from under his eyelids. He then remembered what his father had said. Hesitantly, he loosened the vine fastening on the rucksack. Throwing it open, he peered inside, before sighing and collapsing onto the floor.

"Yes, yes!" he cried.

He jumped to his feet and leapt around the room. Catching his breath, he looked into the rucksack once again. His heart pounded, he smiled, then pulled from it a pair of gleaming new trainers.

CHAPTER 4

"Hello and welcome to Channel eighty-five, *Insect Live*. We are coming to you from Green Leaf Stadium. For those of you who are watching for the first time, I'm Beetle Bob."

"And I'm Louise Ladybird."

"So, Louise, it's almost here. The first ever seven-day mile attempt."

"I know, Bob, I can hardly believe it – a mile in seven days. It's never been done before. In a month, maybe, but a week!"

"Yes, Lou, it's slightly bonkers. What makes it all the more unbelievable is that the event is open to molluscs."

"Molluscs? Are you sure?" said Louise through quivering lips.

"If the rumour is true, Lou, if the rumour is true."

"What can we expect to happen over the next seven days, Bob?"

"Even with all their best intentions, I just can't see how a mile in such a short space of time is possible," said Bob, shaking his head.

"Shall we go and meet our adventurous contestants?" asked Lou.

The warped seat on Bob's acorn chair squeaked when he pushed back from the desk. Grabbing his sunglasses, he stood up and took Lou by the hand. Leaving the studio together, they weaved through a maze of narrow corridors onto the stage.

"Please put your antennae and legs together for your hosts, Bob Beetle and Louise Ladybird," announced the producer.

"Wow!" said Lou, as the spectators clapped and cheered. "Unbelievable, what a crowd!"

"Thank you, thank you, and thank you," said Bob.

Bob and Lou stood back and gazed at the mass of fans that filled the stadium.

"Well, do you want to meet the contestants? Well, do you?" said Bob.

With a rolled-up leaf pressed to her lips, an ant from the tenth row screamed, "Yeah, Yeah."

Cheers and screams echoed through the stadium.

Boom, boom.

Everyone in the stadium grasped their ears, as a huge puff of smoke slipped over the stage. Slowly peeking through the wall of smoke were five empty chairs made from twisted sticks. The stadium fell into darkness. Whispers came from the crowd.

"I can't believe there are five."

"I thought finding one contestant would be a miracle, but five – that's just nuts."

The spotlights turned on, shrouding Bob and Lou in bright light.

"So, here we go, time to meet your first contestant," said Bob.

Archie sat with his legs crossed, watching the light creep over the stage to encompass him. Putting a finger in his mouth, he shuffled back in his chair as Bob and Lou walked towards him.

"Hello and welcome to the show. What's your name?" asked Lou.

Archie tried to reply, but every time he opened his mouth nothing came out.

"Hello, don't you know what your name is?" asked Bob.

The crowd laughed.

"He could be a little nervous," suggested Lou.

"Archie," he whispered.

"What did he say? Did you hear him, Lou?"

Lou and Bob looked at each other and shrugged.

"Could you repeat that?" asked Lou.

Archie took a deep breath. "My name's Archie."

"Good! Good, welcome, Archie."

"It's time to meet our second contestant," announced Bob.

Archie watched the light widen and noticed a pair of pincers pressing into the stage. Sprawled on the second chair was a centipede. He was dull black in colour, with a vibrant yellow stripe running up and down the length of his body.

"Hello and welcome to the show," said Lou.

"Enough of the chit-chat, my name's Snide! Look at my strong legs." Snide leaned forward, tensing his legs to show his bulging muscles.

Archie watched Bob lift his arms, shake his head and turn to Lou.

"Oi, you," said Snide.

Archie turned to see red and yellow eyes staring straight at him.

"Ha! Two legs, you must be joking – that's ninety-eight too few," stated Snide.

Not knowing what to say, Archie turned from Snide's relentless gape to hear Bob address the crowd.

"It's time to meet contestant number three."

"Hello and welcome to the show," said Lou.

Bob put his hand in front of his mouth, laughed and said, "It's true, a mollusc!"

"Why hello, I'm the Professor, otherwise known as the Prof."

Archie noticed a large grey moustache and bushy eyebrows, and he also clocked a discreet window in the side of his big shell. *It can't be the snail who was pushed up the hill*, he thought. *How can he be in the race?*

"How do you think you can compete against, well . . . basically, legs, Prof, legs?" asked Lou.

"The boffins and I have been hard at work in the lab for many seasons," announced the Prof, "and we have a secret formula. It's called Quick Slick!"

"Quick Slick?" repeated Bob. "What does it do?"

"It gives us speed, Bob. No longer will it be said 'as slow as a snail'. Soon it will be 'as fast as one.'"

Laughter echoed around the stadium walls. On and on and on it went.

"Fast as a snail, never," said a caterpillar in the crowd.

The Prof slid from his chair, reached up with his hand-like tentacles and pressed down on a lever connected to a shell-shaped canister. "I'll show them," he mumbled. He retracted his body and zoomed between Bob and Lou, sending them spinning in opposite directions.

Sitting on the back row, covered from wing to toe in thick dust, was an old moth. Sucking in a mouthful of dust, she coughed and then said, "I . . . I don't believe it."

Bob stopped spinning and grasped his wobbling head. "Wow! How about that?" he said.

Lou staggered to Bob and took a deep breath. "It must be the science, astonishing, just astonishing. A round of applause for, dare I say it, the Professor of Speed."

The Prof bowed at the crowd and on the way back to his chair waved with both antennae aloft.

The lights widened to reveal what looked like an empty chair.

"Oh, there you are," said Bob. "Hello and welcome."

"Oh, hello, Bob. It's a pleasure to meet you. Well, my name is Vic the Stick."

Bob pointed to the Prof. "Like the Prof, your species aren't exactly known for speed."

"Well, I have these," replied Vic, pulling from his bag a shiny roller skate with bright red wheels.

"Whatever next, a space hopper?" said Lou.

"Oh, don't be like that, Lou," said Vic, "it doesn't say anything in the rules."

"He's right, Lou," said Bob. "We do only have the three rules. One: follow the arrows, two: only travel between sunrise and sunset, and three: no winged flight."

"Told you," Vic said, looking at Lou.

"It's time to meet contestant number five," announced Bob.

The crowd cheered and the lights widened once again. Sitting with both arms and legs crossed was a female alien.

"There's another one!" announced Lou.

"It's like locusts," declared Bob, looking back at Archie. "You can go all season without seeing one and then you see two in the same day. What next, a swarm?"

"Hello and welcome. What's your name?" asked Lou.

"My name's Fifi."

Archie heard a soft voice and turned to look, but Snide's back blocked his view. He pulled himself forward and, with his head on his knees, spotted his fellow contestant.

"Wow, she's beautiful!"

"Who said that?" asked Bob, looking to his left.

Archie sat back whilst Snide, the Prof and Vic looked at each other.

"Can we have a replay?" asked Bob into his microphone.

Archie blinked. On the big screen, for all to see, was the replay.

The words, "Wow, she's beautiful!" echoed around the stadium.

Knowing he'd been found out, Archie slumped in his chair. Looking at his feet, a warm feeling rolled up his face, turning his antennae slightly pink.

"It was Archie!" Lou declared, turning to Bob, as laughter spilled from her mouth.

Leaning forward, Fifi gave Archie a look that could freeze even the largest of bonfires. "Tut," she uttered, before throwing down her hand and turning away.

"Could love be in the air?" asked Bob.

"I'm here for the running, Bob," declared Fifi. "I've been preparing for this for a long, long time."

"I think we ought to leave it there," said Lou.

The lights faded and, looking from his chair, Archie watched Bob and Lou walk away, still shrouded in bright light.

CHAPTER 5

"So, Lou, is this where you leave me?"

"Yes, Bob, I'm afraid so."

"Please tell the audience where you are going."

"I'm going over to Channel Eighty-Five's *Eye in the Sky* to report on the courageous adventure."

Over to Lou's right came a flash, as the whole stage lit up.

"Oooh, aaaah, that's amazing!" murmured the crowd.

Airship One, an intricate spider's web jam-packed with feathery white dandelion seeds, hovered above the stage. Suspended beneath, by woven silkworm threads, was a wooden cabin, its portholes glinting in the stadium lights. Catching a gust of wind, the seeds gently pushed against the web, moving the spectacular vessel upwards.

"It's absolutely marvellous, Lou, it really is, but do you really expect it to fly?" asked Bob.

"Not only will it fly, Bob, it'll soar high above fields and houses."

"But surely it can only go in the same direction as the wind."

"We have propellers piloted by Captain Cricket and his crew," Lou explained, looking up. "But, I'm not sure how to get up there."

On board, the Captain kicked a coiled ladder made from plaited grass cuttings off the deck. It plunged to the stage with a crash. Bob, slow to react, jumped back. "Be careful up there," he yelled. "Did you see that, Lou, he did that on purpose!"

"Oh, I'm sure he wouldn't do that," replied Lou.

The lights faded, immersing the stadium in darkness, except for one spotlight that focused on Lou. Swinging her hips, she walked to the ladder and wrapped her legs around the rungs. As the ladder retracted and Airship One left the stadium, she waved to the crowd.

37

CHAPTER 6

Backstage, Archie jogged on the spot whilst he looked at the others, who were also warming up for the race. The Prof was sliding back and forth and Vic seemed to be doing press-ups. Fifi stretched.

"What's he doing?" Archie said, as he spotted Snide disappear into the shadows. "That's strange!"

On stage, Bob looked to the sky above the stadium. "Are you there, Lou? Can you hear me?"

"Yes, Bob, loud and clear," replied Lou aboard Airship One.

"How long before sunrise?" asked Bob.

"We're estimating ten minutes before the sunlight hits the coloured light tunnels."

"Understood, contestants to the start." Bob then turned to address the crowd. "Can you believe it, ten minutes to go."

Standing on their seats, the crowd cheered.

"Come on, move it, two legs," said Snide.

Archie shuddered. He'd never felt like this before.

He stumbled forward. As he approached the starting line, he bit his bottom lip. His legs wobbled and his knees clattered.

Snide encircled Archie, but before Archie had the chance to speak, a warm, pungent smell wafted in his face.

"You're not going to win," said Snide. "In fact, I can see you falling flat on your face."

"That's what you think." Archie said, gasping for breath. "My two legs can match all of yours."

"Don't make me laugh!" said Snide, flaring his nostrils before swaggering away.

❉❉❉

"What's that?" Bob held his hand against his ear. "Three more contestants. Are you sure?"

"Yes," replied the producer. "A grasshopper called Gerald, a cockroach called Mildred and a larva by the name of Cecil."

At that moment, the trio appeared on the starting line.

"Sorry, no time to meet you, but welcome," said Bob.

Archie looked over to see a grasshopper wearing a blue flat cap, a wrinkly cockroach with ginormous bulging eyes and a larva precariously perched on top of a grape.

Chapter 7

Where's he going? Archie wondered, as he watched Snide tiptoe from the starting line and stoop down behind Cecil. Then, hearing a tap on a microphone, he looked towards the stage.

"To all you bugs, grubs and slugs, either here in the stadium or watching at home," said Bob, "we're minutes, maybe seconds away from the first ever attempt at a mile in seven days. It's just amazing! How are we looking up there, Lou?"

Lou followed the stream of light from the rising sun, which was rushing along the ground towards the stadium.

"Oh, oh, it's hit the base!" yelled Lou. "It's over to you, Bob."

"Thank you," shrieked Bob. "Quick, contestants, on your marks . . ."

Poised for a quick start, all the contestants fixated on the starting lights.

"There's red, get ready," screeched Bob. "It's amber! It's green! Go, go!"

Fifi, who was first to react, took a massive stride forward. She was followed by Vic, who pushed off using the stoppers on his skates. Close behind was Snide, who sprang over the line. Mildred was slow to start but then scurried off, followed by the hopping Gerald.

Archie leapt forward and crashed to the floor. "Oh no, what's happened?" he cried, while lying flat on his face.

The Prof swivelled his head and saw Archie sprawled out on the track. "Oh dear, are you alright?"

"I'm . . . I'm okay, keep going." He rolled over, rubbed his knees and, as he sat up, spied a quadruple knot between his trainers. "How did that happen?" he wondered out loud.

Boing! Boing! Boing!

Archie looked up to see Cecil springing down the track while perched on top of the grape. He bounced a few times more and then there was an almighty squeak. The track trembled. A plume of juice and air shot from beneath the grape, rocketing it skyward.

Vroom!

The grape almost reached the clear blue sky above the stadium, before it slowed to a stop. Cecil screamed and turned whiter than normal as the fruit began to plummet back towards the arena. It made a whistling sound, which was followed by a loud splat.

"I can't look," mumbled the crowd in varying tones.

Archie screwed up his face and peered through the gap between his fingers. First came the sound of shuffling then a squelch. Cecil's head popped up from a medley of grape pieces.

"He's okay, he's alive," Archie bellowed.

"First Aid to the track! First Aid to the track!" screamed Bob.

Archie turned from Cecil and gazed across the stadium. Fifi entered the tunnel, closely followed by Vic, the Prof, Gerald, Snide and Mildred. They were all jostling for prime position.

Archie tried to undo the extremely tight knot in his laces. "Argh!" he cried, before shaking his head. "I'll never catch up now, it's just too tight." He sighed and allowed his shoulders to slump as his hands fell from the knot.

He stared down at the track. "Maybe I won't finish after all," he said out loud.

"You can do it, Archie, don't give up," said Bob, looking over his sunglasses.

Archie's heavy eyes, drooping mouth and quivering top lip filled the big screen.

Turning to the crowd, Bob raised his hands and they began chanting, "Archie! Archie! Archie! Archie!"

Archie grabbed his laces and sucked in a breath. The knots finally came loose. "I've done it, I've done it!" he cried. Tying the laces tight, he jumped up and started down the track.

CHAPTER 8

Archie ran from the tunnel and began the rampage down Green Leaf Way.

Zipping through Corner Four, his feet started to stomp louder. "Ah . . . ah . . . ah . . . ah," vibrated from his mouth.

Leaning back, he tried to slow down, but on the next turn his feet tangled. He stumbled, plunged forward and watched his legs fly over his head.

Rolling to a stop, he looked over to the clock tower and saw Vic and the Prof making their way into Expectation Avenue.

"I must be five metres behind," he said out loud. He frowned, got to his feet and then ran as fast as possible before entering the square, which was filled with spectators.

"Go, Archie, go," screamed a grasshopper, who was sitting on her father's shoulders.

Archie waved and ran under the clock tower towards the mansions that lined the avenue.

Hours passed, and with the mansions far behind, Archie spotted two old moths. They were sitting together on a porch, in a rocking chair made for two.

He followed the arrows and turned into Anguish Street, only to spot Snide and Fifi disappear over a humpback bridge. "Yes, I'm catching up with them," he declared.

Only a metre behind, Archie quickened his pace and soon ran over the bridge.

Where had they gone? He stopped and looked from the top of the bridge. With no one in sight, he shrugged and sprinted off. Running alongside a vast pebble wall that bent to the left and went on for what seemed like ages, Archie wondered whether he had missed a turn.

He stretched out his neck and stared ahead. *It can't be, that's a dead end, isn't it?* He came to a stop, sighed and looked all around. "What's that?" he asked out loud.

Taking a few steps back, he grabbed hold of a leaf stem and pulled hard. "That's the way," he said. "But who has hidden the arrow under a leaf?"

CHAPTER 9

Archie followed the arrow to two gates. He ran through them and under a sign that read, 'The Honey Factory'. Then, halfway up a cobbled drive, he watched a silhouette disappear into the shadows. *Who's that?* he wondered.

He rounded a corner and The Honey Factory came into sight, its dark walls and bellowing chimneys filling the horizon. Slowing to a walk, he passed a stack of barrels in front of a ramp leading into the building.

It can't be in there, can it? Looking for any other possible route, he noticed an arrow painted on the ramp. Shaking his head, he took a deep breath, edged up to the ramp and peered through the open door. In the black void, he could see a candle flickering in the distance. Then, holding his hands aloft, he ran into the gloom.

Far into the factory, Archie heard a deep rumble. "What's that noise?" he asked out loud.

Sssccrrr . . . sssccrrr.

It got louder and louder.

"What is it, what is it?"

Sssccrrr . . . Sssccrrr.

Closer and closer it sounded.

Biting his lip, Archie glared into the murkiness. Staring at the flickering candle, he glimpsed an ominous shape emerging from the shadows.

Sssccrrr . . .

"Argh, argh!" Archie screamed and launched himself out of the way.

S-s-s-c-c-r-r-r . . . bang!

Archie looked up, flinched and put his arm over his head, as the dancing shadows from the glimmering candle jumped all around him. Holding his breath, he listened. *Shadows, it's only shadows*, he told himself.

Edging forward, he stumbled across a smashed barrel scattered across the ground. "Phew, it's just an accident, that's all."

≈≈≈

Further inside the factory, Fifi and Snide continued the race.

Occasionally, Snide looked at Fifi and spoke in indistinguishable whispers.

"What, what did you say?" Fifi asked. With no response, she glanced across to see Snide gawping back.

Daylight spilled into the factory from an open door. Through squinted eyes, Snide saw a ramp disappearing under the floor.

"You're doing . . . well," said Snide. "Much better than your friend. What's his name again?"

"Look, he's not my friend, but his name is Archieeeee!" Fifi cried out, as she fell through the air. Her legs collapsed on a shiny ramp and she disappeared under the floor. Sliding faster and faster, Fifi pushed her feet and hands against it.

"Arrghh!" She zoomed off the ramp and landed in a sea of bright yellow pollen.

"What am I going to do now?" Putting her finger to her mouth, Fifi looked around. In the centre of the room was a massive creaking corkscrew, which was transferring pollen to the cauldrons above.

"Oh no," screamed Fifi. The force of the pollen pushed her towards the conveyor. Fighting against the tide, she thrust her arms and legs forward.

Breathing heavily, Fifi reached the ramp and on her tiptoes lifted her right knee and pushed herself up with both hands, getting to her feet.

"Woah!" Her legs disappeared over her head and she landed back in the pollen with a plop.

"That's it, I'm out of the race. I'm never going to leave the City now."

Meanwhile, Archie heard his name being shouted and sprinted through the factory. "Hello, hello. Is anybody down there?" he shouted.

"Yes! Help, help, I'm down here," said Fifi, who was floating on the pollen and flapping her arms. She managed to get to her feet and grasp the ramp. "I'm here, I'm here."

Archie looked down the ramp, then to the open door just a short distance away. "Hmmm, hmmm," he said, before heading to the door.

"Are you there, are you there?" shouted Fifi.

With no reply, Fifi's head dropped.

Above, Archie zig-zagged back to the ramp, clutching a fire hose made from daffodil stems. Taking a deep breath, he flung the hose, sending it rattling down the ramp.

"Yes, yes!" cried Fifi, watching the hose clatter into view.

She stretched and stretched some more. When she was a mere fingernail's distance away, she jumped and grabbed the hose with both hands. "Pull, pull!" she shouted.

Taking one arm over the other, Archie did as instructed.

Clinging to the hose nozzle, Fifi slipped from one side of the ramp to the other. Nearing the top, the sound of the constantly grating corkscrew was drowned out by a wheezy whistle.

"Who or what is that?" said Fifi. Stretching her neck, she slipped and, scrambling to her feet, looked over the ramp's crest to see Archie's now purple face.

"Oh, it's you, is it?" Fifi said, stepping from the ramp.

A bead of sweat ran down Archie's face. Gasping for breath, he crumbled onto the cold factory floor and looked at the ceiling. Fifi appeared and gazed down at him. "Thanks," she said.

Archie hadn't uttered a single word before Fifi turned and ran towards the door.

"You're welcome," he mumbled, getting to his feet.

Leaving The Honey Factory, Archie sprinted down a grass runway and quickly caught up with Fifi, who was weaving between the daisies for a centre line.

"Great pace," said Archie.

"Yes, it is."

They ran into a freshly cut meadow, the mauve sky looming ever closer. Running up a gradient, they passed piles of stacked flowers and grasses, before coming to a stop under a willow tree.

Archie brushed away some dirt from a fallen branch.

"Would you like to sit here, Fifi?"

"No!" she replied, sitting on the opposite end.

"Oh, well I guess I'll sit on my own, then."

Fifi and Archie sat in silence and watched the sun slowly fall behind the horizon. The glow of vibrant reds and oranges from the dimming sun filled the surrounding clouds.

Archie lay down and, using a clump of grass for a pillow, watched the sky become darker, before drifting off to sleep.

Chapter 10

Archie stretched out and spoke whilst mid-yawn. "Morning, did you sleep well?" he asked Fifi.

"Yes! And if we are going to run together, we need to get going!"

Taking it in turns to lead, the two competitors swiftly headed down the hill and towards the cornfield below. As Archie ran, he gazed at the dew droplets, which sparkled in the morning sun like jewels.

But who's that? he wondered. Archie noticed a menacing-looking yellow streak reflected on the dew drops, before it faded away.

Leaving the meadow, the tall, thick corn stems reached high into the sky and blocked out the sun. Fifi and Archie ran through the gloom, passing a group of worker ants who were using a winch to collect corn and lower it into a cart that was pulled by a giant woodlouse.

After hours of running through the field, Fifi cried, "I've got to stop, I've got to stop."

She covered her eyes from the sunlight breaking through the canopy, before crashing to the ground.

"What's wrong?" asked Archie.

She yanked off one of her trainers and out fell a jagged stone.

Whilst waiting for her to get sorted, Archie noticed an orange haze falling through the distant corn.

"What's that?" he said out loud. He ran to a disused winch and began to climb the towering corn stem. Clinging to the top, Archie looked over the field to see a dense orange smog moving towards him.

"I know what this is, it's a, er . . . er."

Suddenly, a colossal black object with twelve revolving propellers burst from the haze.

"There it is!" yelled Archie. "It's the human's Insectadrone. Hide, hide, insecticide."

Archie's cries echoed through the field. Further ahead, Snide tried to squeeze into an enclave of stones. He squirmed and, pushing backwards, saw Gerald cocooned under a leaf.

"There's not enough room in here," said Snide. He wriggled free and charged forward.

"Ouch!" screamed Gerald, as he came crashing to the floor.

"Ha, good luck! No room in here!" Snide pulled on the leaf, concealing him inside.

Gerald retracted his legs and took a huge leap. "Ow!" he cried.

Whilst in mid-air, the orange mist had covered his legs, but, undeterred by the pain, he hopped away.

❤❤❤

Archie abseiled down the corn and ran to Fifi, but she wasn't there. He looked to his left, right and then spun round. *Oh, where is she?*

Archie turned again and saw Fifi gracefully jump over a rock and casually duck under a leaf. "She's amazing," he muttered.

Landing at Archie's side, Gerald grabbed his leg. "Run, boy, run."

"What, what's that?" Archie asked, looking at Gerald's smouldering legs. "Let me help you."

"You need to run, boy, run."

Archie sprinted forward, then stopped. Grabbing a leaf with both hands, he pulled it towards Gerald and covered him with it. Leaving him safely cocooned, he started after Fifi.

A sound similar to falling rain grew louder and moved ever closer. Too scared to look back, Archie focused forward, jumping over rocks and stooping under leaves. He approached a steep dyke and, with no time to think, leapt forward.

"Argh!"

Landing on a long, winding leaf, Archie began to slide, picking up speed as he went.

Close to the bottom of the dyke, Archie shot off the end leaf then came to a stop. He lunged forward before starting to pirouette.

"Oh no! Argh!"

He stumbled, and with the orange mist close to brushing his lips, slammed his eyes shut.

Chapter 11

"Welcome to our special report. Let's go live to Airship One, which is currently hovering over Willow Meadow.

"Hello, Lou. Can you tell us what's happening?"

"Yes, Bob, we can see the orange mist slowly dispersing from the field."

"And what about some type of rescue?" asked Bob.

"Emergency crews are still metres away. We have been told we won't know anything until the morning."

Bob shuffled some papers. "Thank you, Lou. Folks, you've heard it here first, on Channel eighty-five *Insect Live*. Good evening."

CHAPTER 12

"Good morning," said Lou. "Reports have been coming in that so far there have only been superficial injuries following the Insectadrone attack. A woodlouse has a sprained ankle, a caterpillar turned orange from eating a contaminated leaf and a group of ants appear to have something resembling mild sunburn."

"And any news on the contestants?" asked Bob.

"I'm afraid not, we just don't know at this time."

"Antennae and legs crossed, I think," replied Bob.

"I'm Louise Ladybird. Goodbye for now."

"And goodbye from the studio," added Bob.

CHAPTER 13

The sun surged down the dyke and into a can. Woken by the light, Archie opened his eyes to see his reflection staring back. "Wow," he said. "But how did I get in here?"

"You fainted and I pulled you in," replied Fifi.

Archie thanked his new friend and got to his feet. "What's that over there?" he asked. "It . . . it looks like coloured water."

"And it bubbles like it's hot," Fifi replied.

Archie walked to the end of the can, bowed down and then plunged his cupped hands into the liquid. He puckered his lips and took a sip. His tongue hissed, fizzed and, as he smiled, a bubble crept from between his lips and popped. "Mmmm, I've never had such a drink."

Grabbing Archie's cupped hands, Fifi took a sip. "It tickles from the inside," she said, rubbing her nose.

Opening his mouth to reply, Archie burped. "I like this!" he said with a chuckle, before drinking some more. "I feel I could run to the end of the world."

"Me too!" replied Fifi.

Leaping from the can, they ran along the flat of the dyke and up to the long row of corn. After a few minutes, they heard a voice coming from the back of an ambulance cart.

"Hey, boy! Boy!"

Archie turned and then came to a stop. It was Gerald.

"I'm glad you're safe, Gerald," Archie said. Then he looked down and saw bandages wrapped around his fellow competitor's legs. "Oh, no!"

Gerald took Archie's hand and looked up. "Not to worry," he said. "Only a few singed hairs. Now get running, you have a race to finish."

The field seemed never ending, and, after many hours of running, Archie and Fifi took a break.

Sitting with his back pressed against a corn stem, Archie gasped for breath. "I don't know about running to the end of the world," he said. "This field is bad enough!"

After a few minutes, Fifi stood up. In front of her was an arrow etched in the dry mud. "It's this way, Archie," she said.

Archie stood up and followed Fifi to a ginormous hedge.

"Just look at those," Archie said, pointing at hundreds of serrated thorns hanging from every twisted branch. They crept forward and into the contorted maze. Bent under a low branch, Fifi started to stand.

"Stop, stop!" shouted Archie.

A split second from impaling herself, Fifi froze.

Crouching down again, she turned her head and saw the blood-stained, fang-like thorn.

"Thank you," she said, scrambling clear of the hedge.

Archie crawled under the last branch and saw four distinct trails winding up a hill.

"They look fresh," he said. "I think we're catching up with the others."

On their hands and knees, Archie and Fifi clambered up the hill.

Later that day, the pair approached the summit, as a cloud-like mist rolled over the brow and towards them.

"What's that?" said Archie.

Something illuminated the smog, turning it an eerie yellow.

"What is it, what is it?" yelled Fifi.

Poking through the slowly clearing haze was a bright yellow sign carved from a piece of corn.

"Compostonberry," read Archie.

"What's Compostonberry?"

"I've heard that it's a pile of steaming compost, and it's the venue for the annual Slug Fest."

"Slugs, they're just too slimy!" said Fifi.

The mist cleared and the pair ran until the sun began to set. Stopping under a gigantic red toadstool high on a rim, Archie looked down and into an arena.

"Look, Fifi."

In the middle of an empty arena, curled up on a decomposing cucumber, was Snide. Meanwhile, Vic, the Prof and Mildred were in the otherwise empty VII (Very Important Insect) area.

CHAPTER 15

The next day, woken by the sound of pounding rain, Archie rolled from under a leaf. Getting to his feet, he heard someone knocking against the window of the Prof's shell. From under the toadstool, he looked into the arena and saw Vic exposed to the elements, with rain bouncing off his head. A moment later, the Prof appeared from under his shell clasping a brolly.

Distracted, the Prof looked to his right. Standing motionless, with rain running into his eyes, was Snide.

Snide stared without blinking, turned up his lip and then scurried away.

"Ghastly, just ghastly," whispered Vic, as they too got back in the race.

Archie stepped into the pelting rain and skidded. One of his legs shot into the air. Regaining his balance, he looked at Fifi, who clung to the side of a carrot. "It will take us hours to get down that slimy, rotten, muddy vegetable slope," he said, shuffling backwards.

Fifi looked the carrot up and down and then clambered on board. "Well, are you coming?" she asked, grasping hold of the green tops, which were like reins.

Archie peered into the arena, frowned, shrugged and turned out his hands. "I guess so."

He sat behind Fifi and the pair rocked the carrot back and forth until it juddered and then slid over the muddy slick.

"Here we go! Hold on!" yelled Fifi, just as the carrot came to a stop.

Teetering over the edge of the rim, the carrot creaked. Then, without warning, the back of the vegetable shot into the air and they plummeted downwards.

"Argh! Argh!" Fifi and Archie screamed.

Zooming past the black, Wellington boot-shaped stage, they headed out of the arena, passing a sign that read, "Green Leaf Stadium Half a Mile."

Archie smiled. He had never travelled so far.

The rain ran off the chaotic mixture of rotting vegetables that lined the route from Compostonberry. Turning a corner, Archie looked ahead and saw Vic thrusting a piece of straw between the wheels of his skates. "Hello," he shouted, as they passed.

"Oh, hello," replied the Prof, peering from under his brolly.

"What did you say, Prof?" asked Vic.

"Just saying hello to Fifi and Archie."

"Oh no, we're last," sniffled Vic. "All I want is to be famous, and no one is ever famous for being last, are they?"

"Don't worry," said the Prof, as he watched the last of the rain clouds float off. "This sludge will soon dry up."

"More speed, more speed," whispered Archie. "We can win, Fifi, we can win."

Leaning forward, they passed Mildred over a crest.

Halfway down the slope, Snide was planning his own victory. "If we win, we'll tie up the Captain and steal the airship," he said. "Ha, ha, ha!"

Leaving Compostonberry behind, Archie and Fifi, still on board the carrot, zoomed down the slope. As they overtook Snide, Fifi tugged the reins, sending a shower of thick brown sludge over him. He skidded to a stop and wiped his face. Shaking off the muck from his legs, he looked down the slope. "Argh, who was that?" he asked.

The ground flattened and, thinking their slalom-type ride was over, Fifi released the reins. The carrot glided towards the allotments and the glistening Beck Canyon beyond.

"Can you believe it, we're in the lead!" said Fifi.

Before Archie could reply, the carrot hit an

unforgiving ramp and launched them into the air and towards a precipice.

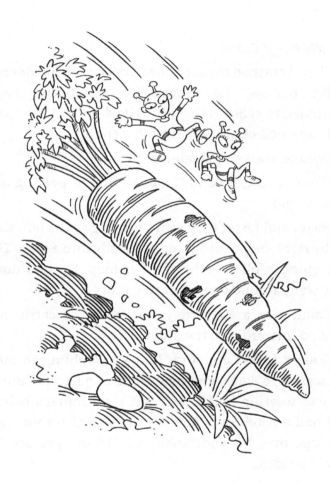

CHAPTER 15

Crunch! Bang! Crack!

They'd crashed through the barrier of an abandoned rabbit burrow. The sound of splintering twigs continued to echo up the hill, as daylight quickly faded and the smell of old, wet fur filled the air.

"Where are we?" screamed Fifi.

"I'm not sure, hold on!" replied Archie, peering into a black void.

Faster and faster they went, turning to the left, then to the right, before dropping vertically into a loop. This was quickly followed by another loop. Up and down they went around a maze of tree roots.

Coming to a stop, they slid from the carrot and strolled forward into the gloom.

Lost and tired and after hours of ambling through the warren, a worm emerged from an adjacent tunnel. He was wearing half a hazelnut for a miner's helmet and had a patch over one eye. He was also sporting a bandage over his shortened tail. "Didn't you see the sign?" he said.

Archie and Fifi looked at each other, shrugged and replied, "Sign, what sign?"

The worm looked up and down the tunnel.

"Not to worry, maybe it will be OK," he said. "You must be Archie and Fifi. My name's Wally. It's not safe to stop here, so follow me!"

They followed the worm. After a short distance, the

aroma of slow-cooked vegetables filled the tunnel. It was then that Archie saw a warm glow coming from an open door.

"Come in, come in," said Wally, pushing against the thick, dark-panelled door. Its rusty hinges creaked before the door shut with a clunk.

Archie and Fifi looked around the lavishly styled room. The walls and ceilings were made from dark granite and the floor was carpeted with a thick, lush moss.

"Welcome to my headquarters," boasted Wally. "Help yourselves." He nodded in the direction of a lava stone with a clay pot suspended above it.

Archie and Fifi gazed at a steaming vegetable casserole. Fifi's tongue rolled over her lips in anticipation of the creamy tomato stock that smothered succulent vegetables of all shapes and sizes. "This will give us extra energy for tomorrow," she said.

"I'm not even sure that we're still on the route," Archie admitted, lowering his head and looking at the floor.

"Ah, well, that's something I can help you with," said Wally. He wriggled into his robotic arms and moved to a pole in the centre of the room. Pulling some handles, a periscope popped out in the allotment above, through the top of an onion stem. "Now, let's have a look," he said and moved the pole around. "That's Compostonberry, there's the setting sun, and that's the way over to Beck Canyon. So you're still en route."

Archie smiled and lifted his head. "Did you hear that, Fifi, we can still do it. We're not out of the race yet."

"Sit down and eat up," said Wally. "You have an early start tomorrow."

CHAPTER 16

Archie woke and, after moving aside Wally's loose bandage, which was draped over his legs, carefully slid from the sofa. Wally snored and snored again before opening his good eye. "What, what's happening?" he said. He stretched out his tail, shook his robotic arms and moved to the periscope. "No time to waste, all clear above – let's go, let's go!"

Wally lit the lamp on his helmet before ushering Archie and Fifi out of the door and into the tunnel. "I'll show you the way to go, then I must go back," he said.

"Okay, Wally, and thank you for your help," said Archie.

"Did you hear that?" asked Fifi.

"What, silence?" Archie said, turning out his hands and frowning.

"No, listen, just listen," said Fifi, placing her head against the wall of the tunnel. "And did you feel that?"

"Feel what?" asked Wally.

"The ground, it trembled."

Wally shone his torch up and down the tunnel. "Are you sure? It was clear above."

"Yes, there it is again. Did you feel that?"

"I did, I did," said Archie.

Wally glided backwards and forwards. "I'm not sure, I'm just not sure," he said.

The ground shook, whilst huge clumps of the ceiling crashed onto the floor, covering them in dust and clumps of mud.

"Is it an earthquake?" hollered Archie.

"Worse, much worse! It's a gardener!" screamed Wally.

A thunderous rumble echoed through the tunnel, followed by the sound of fracturing ground.

"Which way, Wally, which way?" shrieked Fifi.

"That way," said Wally, pointing away from the noise.

The ground trembled and, staggering from one side of the tunnel to the other, Archie stooped, thrust down a hand and looked over his shoulder to see Wally several paces behind. "Come on, Wally," he roared.

A shiny silver spade crashed through the ceiling, tearing the tunnel in two. Blown to the ground, Archie watched the shimmering spade burst back through the soil, lifting him and Fifi high into the air.

"What now?" screamed Fifi.

Archie grabbed her hand. "Quick, jump," he shouted.

With their eyes clamped shut, they jumped at the same time. Tumbling, Fifi squealed. The wind shrieked past, as Archie aimlessly flapped his arms and kicked out his legs before landing, feet first, in a soft heap of straw. "Yes, yes, we made it!" he said, getting to his feet. He jumped up and down, sucking in the sweet-scented air of the allotment and smiling.

But where was Wally?

Archie looked at the shattered tunnel strewn across the ground. "Oh no," he said, as his smile disappeared and he covered his mouth.

But then he looked around and saw Wally's silhouette moving across the allotment and out of harm's reach.

CHAPTER 17

Fifi and Archie followed four fresh tracks towards Beck Canyon, stopping after they'd passed the last allotment.

"Oh no, how are we going to get across now?" said Archie.

Blowing in the wind, he had seen the remains of a majestically weaved straw bridge. Each time it clattered against the wall, more of the bridge disintegrated and fell into the stream below.

Archie peered up and down the canyon then pointed ahead. "Look, there's Mildred," he said.

Fifi and Archie watched the rescue team move towards their fellow competitor, who was clinging to a piece of the bridge.

"That's it, we're out of the race with Mildred," said Fifi, as a stream of warm tears made tracks down her face.

"I'm not giving up," said Archie. "I can't finish like this. We've come too far. We might be on the wrong side of the canyon, but maybe we can find another way to cross it."

Fifi and Archie seemed to run for hours. Then, looking over the empty ravine, Archie saw four silhouettes. Vic and the Prof looked to be in first and second place. Then what appeared to be Snide was in third and fourth.

How's that possible? Archie wondered. He rubbed his eyes and then watched two silhouettes become one. *I must be tired,* he decided.

CHAPTER 18

"Good evening, and welcome to the report on day five. Hello, Lou, are you there?"

"Yes, Bob, and with the mysterious collapse of the bridge over Beck Canyon, it's been a dramatic day."

"And what about the remaining contestants?"

"Three have a small chance to complete the race, but Archie and Fifi are as good as finished, with no way to cross the canyon."

"Such a shame. Thank you, Lou. It's now time to go to the weather. Hello, Sally."

"Good evening. Tomorrow will be dull and hurricane-force winds are a possibility for day seven. We just don't know yet, the wind could go to the left, to the right, or even straight on."

"Thank you, Sally, and it's good night from me, Beetle Bob."

CHAPTER 19

Waking to a dreary morning, Archie stretched back his arms and walked to the mouth of the canyon. Joined by Fifi, they looked across the tributary and to the lake beyond. They watched vapour rise from the water and meet the grey morning sky. Right in the middle of the horizon, appearing like a vast burning orb, was the sun; its dark orange glow infusing the otherwise gloomy sky.

"Oh, Archie! How can we get to the other side?" asked Fifi.

Archie stared ahead, contemplating all the possible ways to cross. He looked into the sky for inspiration and the answer came into view, as he watched a sycamore helicopter seed gently spin over the expanse of water to the other side.

"That's how we'll get across," said Archie. "We need to climb that tree and jump onto a heli seed. I'm not going to fail. I'm going on a world tour."

They climbed for hours, before stopping for a rest in a vacant woodpecker's house. As Fifi relaxed, Archie looked into the gnarly branches and spotted a perfectly sized heli seed, which was glistening in the afternoon sun.

"That's the one for us," he said.

Straddling the branch, he shuffled forward and lowered himself onto the heli seed. Above, Fifi edged forward. Munching on the branch's last leaf was a big, fat purple-and-orange-spotted caterpillar.

"Hello," Fifi said.

"Sorry, can't talk, must eat," replied the caterpillar, spitting out pieces of leaf.

Fifi shook her head and slid onto the rickety heli seed. "Wh . . . what next?" she asked. Shaking like the leaves above, she thrust her arms around the stalk.

Archie pulled on the stem, but it just wouldn't release. He tugged and tugged, but still the heli seed wouldn't budge. Together, the friends started jumping, which rocked the whole branch.

"It's no good, it just won't move," said Archie, as his chin fell to his chest. But thinking about the mockery he once faced, he declared, "No, I'm not giving up!" His antennae burned red and his whole body trembled. He stamped his foot, grabbed the stem and shook it with all his strength.

"What's going on down there?" garbled the caterpillar.

Archie stopped what he was doing. Fifi was poised to reply when she was covered in a shower of chewed-up leaf pieces, as the caterpillar let out a branch-shaking burp.

Fifi frowned and wiped her face. "If you're still hungry, would you like to nibble on this delicious stem?" she asked.

"Mmmm, I shouldn't really." The caterpillar thought for a second. "But it would make such a nice dessert!"

The caterpillar licked his lips then, without taking a breath, he began gnawing at the stem. "A bit chewy," he mumbled between mouthfuls.

Crunch! Crack! The heli seed fell free of the branch.

"Thanks," yelled Archie.

Grasping the stem, Fifi slipped her clammy palms over Archie's. Buffeted from side to side, her eyes grew wider the closer they got to the ground. Fearing a crash, she screamed. Then a small gust of wind started the heli seed spinning. It hovered above the ground before flying up and towards the tributary.

An hour later, bathed in the warm glow of the sun, the heli seed slowed and descended towards the shoreline. Archie stood up and watched the water's edge come in and out of view. "No, no, it can't be," he wailed. "It is! Look, Fifi, we've caught them up!"

Heading towards a watermill, Archie looked at Snide, who was standing at the top of several cobbled steps.

"What? Who? No!" yelled Snide. Gawping up, he slipped and tumbled head over pincers.

"Serves you right for pushing me down the ramp!" shouted Fifi.

"Hold on!" yelled Archie.

The ground ever closer, Fifi and Archie grasped the seed's stalk and shut their eyes.

Thud! Bang!

Travelling at speed, the spinning heli seed scattered sparks in every direction. Scraping down the path and through the open gates of the watermill, they overtook

Vic and the Prof before coming to a stop in the middle of a large courtyard.

"Oh my! Where have you two come from?" Vic asked.

Fifi and Archie stepped off the heli seed, staggered around and then collapsed.

"Oh no, what's wrong?" Vic asked.

The Prof looked at the scored marks on the ground. He tapped the side of his face and said, "I'm no medic, but I think dizzy."

"Dizzy, what's dizzy?"

"It's the effect of balance overload," explained the Prof to Vic.

Fifi and Archie stood up and wobbled over to their fellow competitors. Breaking into a group conversation, they were interrupted by Snide, who was standing in the gateway.

"You four make me laugh!" he said. "There's no chance that any of you are going to beat me!" He walked over to one of the many storerooms surrounding the courtyard. Then, taking a final look, he snarled and slammed the door shut.

"He's so mean," said Vic, skating up behind the Prof. "Someone should have a word with his mother!"

The crescent moon peaked over the horizon and together the four retreated to a large storeroom to rest for the night.

Chapter 20

"Good evening, and welcome to this special evening report. With rumours of cheating reverberating around the studio, what will the fate of two of our contestants be? Let's go now to our eye in the sky, Louise. Good evening, Lou. What can you tell us about the pictures that show the apparent use of a rule-breaking wing?"

"Yes, Bob, I'm aware of the rules on winged flight during this race. However, on this technical matter, we need the opinion of an expert who, of course, is our Captain Cricket aboard Airship One."

Holding the ship's wheel, which was carved from a peach stone, the Captain turned to face the camera.

"Good evening, Captain, what is your opinion on the use of a wing?" asked Bob.

"As you know, or should know, the *Bugasaurus* states that the definition of winged flight means, 'An object attached to a body, powered by muscles, leading to controlled flight.'

"Just remind me, Bug, sorry Bob, in what way does the picture in front of you resemble winged flight?"

Bob stared over his glasses at the picture of Fifi and Archie on the heli seed.

"I think that clears up any suspicion of cheating," said Lou.

"Point taken," replied Bob. "Anyway, let's get back to the race. What can we expect tomorrow?"

"Yes, Bob, an exciting day ahead. The route back to the stadium looks straightforward. It's going to be close."

"See you back here in the stadium tomorrow."

"You sure will," replied Lou.

"What will tomorrow bring? Is the unbelievable going to become a reality? Will the mile be completed? I'm Beetle Bob, saying goodnight."

CHAPTER 21

Archie woke up, rubbed his eyes and saw the Prof draw back his curtains and fling open his window.

"Good morning, Archie," he whispered.

Archie stood up. He could only see one of his trainers. He shrugged and tiptoed towards the Prof, slipping as he went. One leg went to the left and the other to the right. "Woah!" he screamed.

"What's all that noise?" said Vic, opening his eyes.

Archie skidded past and smashed into a stack of barrels.

"Am I dreaming?" said Fifi, as one of the containers clattered to the floor.

Slumped over another barrel, Archie gasped for breath. "It's the floor, it's like ice," he said.

"Ice? No, it won't be ice," said the Prof.

"Oh, where is it? Has anybody seen my other skate?"

"And my trainer," uttered Fifi.

"Yours too?" said Archie.

"And that looks like Quick Slick!" said the Prof.

The Prof stretched out his neck and followed the liquid trail from the floor, up his shell and to two puncture marks in the canister. "It's sabotage!" he shouted.

The room fell silent. Then they shouted in unison: "Snide!"

Their antennae hung down as they looked to the floor in silence again.

"Oh, this is stupid," said Archie, "At least one of us should finish."

He walked over, picked up his trainer and offered it to Fifi.

"What do you mean?" she asked.

"You can use my trainer."

"Thank you, I would," she replied, holding her own trainer aloft. "But I don't have two left feet."

"It's all too much," said a tearful Vic.

"Now, now, it's not as bad as all that," said the Prof, giving Vic a one-tentacled hug.

Hearing an ominous noise, Archie looked to the door. It rattled, the hinges creaked and then it burst open. The wind screeched through the dust-filled air, tossing over boxes. Ravaged by the wind, Archie staggered to the door, but it was far too heavy for him to close on his own.

With Fifi's help, Archie eventually managed to shut it. *But how could Snide have opened and closed the door on his own?* Archie shook his head. Then, looking around, he suddenly had an idea! "We've all come too far to give up," he said. "I can't fail, I just can't, but with everyone's help, we can *all* finish today."

"What do you mean?" asked Fifi.

"It's just not possible," said the Prof. "Vic and I are far too slow now."

Vic looked at Archie, his tears pooling over the floor.

"No, just listen!" Archie said.

After he'd finished talking, Vic blew his nose on the Prof's handkerchief. "Are you sure it will work, Archie?" he asked.

"Yes!" Archie replied.

The Prof nodded and mumbled, "Wind speed times the distance . . . yes!"

They dragged the heli seed into the storeroom before starting work.

First, they attached Vic's remaining skate to the front, and two old cartwheels to the back. Then they fixed on some bark to make a platform. Their final task was to make a sail from a collection of leaves that had blown against the door.

CHAPTER 22

Fifi and Archie pushed back the storeroom door and rolled the land yacht into the courtyard.

"To your places," hollered Archie.

Vic and the Prof took their positions at the back, with Fifi taking a seat on Archie's left.

"Let's go," ordered Archie.

Fifi tugged a vine and four green leaves cascaded from the stem, unfolding into a sail. Filled by the wind, the yacht creaked, lurched forward and quickly crossed the courtyard, passing the watermill's enormous wooden wheel. Smashed and mangled within its cogs was a skate and two trainers.

"Prof, did you see that?" said Vic.

"Cheats never prosper," replied the Prof.

Leaving the watermill, they turned right into a wide-open street. Picking up speed, they abruptly veered from one side of the street to the other.

"Steady, Archie, steady!" muttered the Prof.

Archie was heading directly towards a woodlouse.

"Watch out!" screamed Vic.

The woodlouse turned and tipped over a cart, spewing corn over the road. "Get some glasses!" he shouted.

Banging and scraping against the kerb, the yacht approached the turn into Expectation Avenue. Archie swung the bar and the wheels screeched, skidding sideways around the corner. "Look, it's the stadium!" he cried.

Everyone on board smiled, as they spied the magnificent stadium on the horizon.

Clickety-clack, clickety-clack. The wind blew them ever closer to the stadium. Looking around, Archie noticed a reddish tinge to the sky, signalling the start of sunset.

"I think we need a plan if we catch Snide!" he suggested.

After a quick discussion, Archie and Fifi changed places.

Tousled by the wind, Archie stood up and pressed an eye against the hole in the Prof's canister. "There's a drop left," he shouted.

"It might work," replied the Prof.

The yacht rocketed under a clock tower and entered the plaza to the applause of cheering fans.

"You can catch him!" shouted an earwig.

"Go, go, go!" hollered a grasshopper.

"Oh, thank you, thank you," acknowledged Vic.

They zoomed through the plaza and started the ascent of Green Leaf Way. Surging upward, the yacht screeched around each corner.

"Look, there's Snide!" yelled Archie. "To your places."

Vic stretched forward and took hold of the bottom of the sail, whilst the Prof grasped Vic's legs with his antennae.

Fifi started to turn into the last corner.

"Argh!" screamed Vic.

A huge boulder rumbled down the hill, bouncing and crashing towards them.

Fifi abruptly turned the yacht and tipped it on two wheels. The rock bounced past. Landing, the yacht vibrated, twitched and headed towards a mushroom.

"No!" shouted Fifi.

The sail clattered on the mushroom's curved top, showering them in broken lights. They'd certainly slowed down, but luckily they were still going fast enough to turn into the final corner.

"It's Snide, get ready!" yelled Archie.

"Where have you lot come from?" shrieked Snide.

Fifi veered the yacht in front of him and the Prof released the last drop of Quick Slick.

Snide slipped and slid, as all hundred of his legs moved in sequence. Neither moving forwards or back, he ran faster and faster without going anywhere. "Argh!" he screamed.

The yacht took off over the brow and upon landing, Fifi turned back towards Green Leaf Way.

"Now!" shouted Archie.

Vic released the sail and, as the Prof slid from the yacht, he pulled Vic with him.

"Quick!" shouted Fifi.

Archie and Fifi jumped from the yacht and pushed it as fast as possible into Green Leaf Way. Peeping over the crest, Archie saw that Snide was still running on the spot. He was grimacing and green, foaming saliva squirted between the gaps in his crooked yellow teeth.

"Argh!" he yelled again. His expanding eyes pushed back his forehead, as he watched the yacht teeter over the brow.

The yacht hurtled down the hill and slid underneath Snide. One by one his legs were pushed backwards until he was lying flat on his belly. "You, you . . ." he yelped.

A black and yellow streak shot out from behind a rock, dashed through the crowd and jumped in front of the yacht.

"I'll save you, Snide."

Crack!

A hundred legs were pushed back. Lying at Snide's side was his brother, Fetid. They both snarled, "Argh, Argh."

Archie, Fifi, Vic and the Prof watched them both disappear down Green Leaf Way.

"Oh my, there's two of them!" said Vic.

"Identical twins," muttered the Prof.

"They've been sabotaging the race together, starting with my laces, then Cecil, and then . . ." exclaimed Archie.

The glow of vibrant fiery reds from the setting sun filled the whole sky. Taking a final look over the City, Archie turned and together the four remaining contestants made their way towards the stadium tunnel.

"Hello, yes," said Bob. "We're back for the final moments of the first ever seven-day mile. Well, Lou, what a week it's been."

"Yes, Bob, I can hardly believe it, not only has a week

gone by, but we're seconds away from seeing our brave contestants."

The fans' cheers grew louder and louder when four silhouettes came into view from the tunnel. The stadium shook as the vast crowd stood up and cheered and clapped. Never before had such elation been heard.

Archie looked towards the multitude of fans filling the stadium. In the front row, with the biggest beaming smiles of all, were his father, mother, brother Rew and sisters, Ula and Hesta. "I've done it, I've done it," he shouted.

Archie waved and crossed the line with Fifi, closely followed by Vic and the Prof. They turned to the stage and saw Bob, Lou and Captain Cricket gazing at them in admiration.

Bob waited for the crowd to go silent then looked over his sunglasses and lifted his microphone. "You've made the impossible possible. You have set new standards for all slugs, bugs and grubs. We thank you."

"From all of us here at Channel eighty-five *Insect Live*, I'm Louise Ladybird . . ."

"And I'm Beetle Bob. Goodnight."

If you're wondering what has happened to the adventurous contestants or the wonderful presenters, then the next time you're playing in the park or your garden just stop, look and listen – you might just witness the wondrous word of all things creepy, crawly and slimy!

ACKNOWLEDGEMENTS

Writing doesn't come easy to me, so my self-belief and determination make up only part of what led this book to completion.

I'd like to thank all the special people in my life – my family and friends – for my life's journey to date, and for putting up with the constant descriptions of what I was writing during the years it took to finish this book.

The support I received from the most caring, companionate and amazing lady ever – my mum, Joan Lovett – will stay with me for life. How we cried with laughter over Archie's adventures, as we went through the book line by line checking that all-important grammar.

This book would not be the same without the fabulous illustrations undertaken by the talented Ian R Ward. I appreciate all the help and advice that Sandra Glover from Cornerstones Literary Consultancy provided. The efficient and diligent work carried out by Danielle Wrate and her team at Wrate's Editing Services has also been fantastic.